# Little DAYMOND
# LEARNS to EARN

written by
## DAYMOND JOHN

illustrated by
## NICOLE MILES

Random House · New York

It was the best street fair Daymond had ever seen.
So many people! So much for sale!

Luckily, Daymond had helped at his mom's booth earlier. He had worked hard and earned five dollars. His mom had counted out the crisp dollar bills. "One. Two. Three. Four. Five!"

What would he buy?

Daymond saw something amazing . . .
a Minka J poster! His favorite pop star!

MINKA ♩

MINKA ♩

Honestly, she was everyone's favorite.

Daymond put his money down. "One. Two. Three. Four. Five!"
"Sorry, the poster costs ten dollars," the man said.

"Yikes! I don't
have that much."

*What's here?* Daymond thought.

Booths with toys.

Booths with books.

Booths with art supplies.

Booths with . . . friends!

"Come paint! It's only a dollar," Omar said as Imani waved Daymond over to the craft booth.

Daymond didn't want to spend a dollar. And he wanted to keep looking around. But it would be cool to design his own shirt. . . .

*Music!* Daymond had an idea.

"I'm putting a musical note on mine," Layla said, humming a tune.

Let's do it!

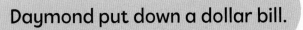

Daymond put down a dollar bill.

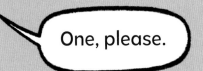

One, please.

Daymond made an amazing Minka J shirt.
But he couldn't stop thinking about the poster.

Now he only had four dollars left.
That meant he needed six more.
How could he earn the rest of the money?

A group of older kids from school walked by.

Daymond thought about it.
"Sure, for five dollars!"

Daymond gave the boy
the T-shirt. The boy
handed Daymond the
money. "One. Two.
Three. Four. Five!"

"I have the greatest business idea EVER!" Daymond said as they raced back to the craft booth. "My mom said to think about what I'm good at and how to use that to solve a problem!"

He put down the money he'd earned from his mom.
"One. Two. Three. Four."

Then he put down the money
he'd earned from the T-shirt sale.
"Five. Six. Seven. Eight. Nine."

The woman at the booth
handed him nine T-shirts.

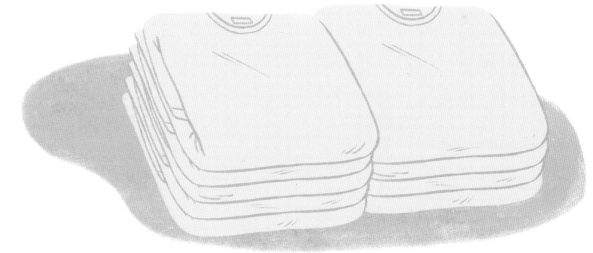

"Let's get to work!" Daymond cheered.

"Now it's time to sell!" Daymond, Layla, Omar, and Imani spread out their shirts for everyone to see.

T-shirts for sale! Five dollars!

The friends watched and waited. . . .

But nobody bought shirts.

"Starting a business is way harder than I thought," Daymond told his mom.

"Your friends helped you make the shirts," she said. "Maybe they can help in other ways. What are they good at?"

Daymond looked around and noticed signs on other booths.

"Omar, can you create a colorful banner?"

"I can see it now!"
Omar drew and painted.

"Layla, can you get people's attention?"

"Let's do this!" Layla marched and
played a Minka J tune on her harmonica.

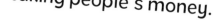
...king people's money.

"I'm dividing my...
a new math bo...

Soon...

...oins. "I'm saving...
...r a tuba. Or a bassoo...

At the end of the day
counted up all the m
was a success! They

Daymond and his friends raced to the poster booth.
Daymond put his money down.
"One. Two. Three. Four. Five. Six. Seven. Eight. Nine. TEN!"

He bought the last Minka J poster . . .

and a brand-new business book.

"I learned so much today," Daymond said.

His mom kissed him good night. "I'm so proud of you. I knew you could do it!"

MINKA ♪

"Maybe tomorrow I'll start an even bigger business with my friends!"

As Daymond's mom turned off the light, she laughed and said, "I know you will, Little Daymond."

# Start Your Own Business

Do you want to make money like Little Daymond and his friends? You can do that by starting your own business. Little Daymond is ready to help. Here's a checklist you can follow:

**Step One:** Think about what you like and are good at. This is *your* special skill.

**Step Four:** Ask your friends to help. Working together is always better.

**Step Two:** Look for a problem that needs to be solved. Now it's time to take action.

**Step Five:** Make sales and decide what to do with the money you make.

**Step Three:** What can you do to solve the problem? This is *your* business.

# What Is Money?

Money looks like this:  and like this:

It is a way to *buy* things you want and *help* other people.

How can you use your money?

**1** **Spend**

You can spend your money on a *product* or *service*.

**2** **Save**

If you want to buy something but you don't have enough money, you can *save* to *buy it later*.

**3** **Donate**

There are lots of organizations that use *donations* to do helpful things.

**4** **Invest**

You can invest your money in stocks, bonds, or cryptocurrency in the hope that they will *increase in value*. *Investment* can also be a way to support companies whose values you agree with.

Congratulations! You can start a business just like Little Daymond! For educational games and activities, check out **LittleDaymond.com**.

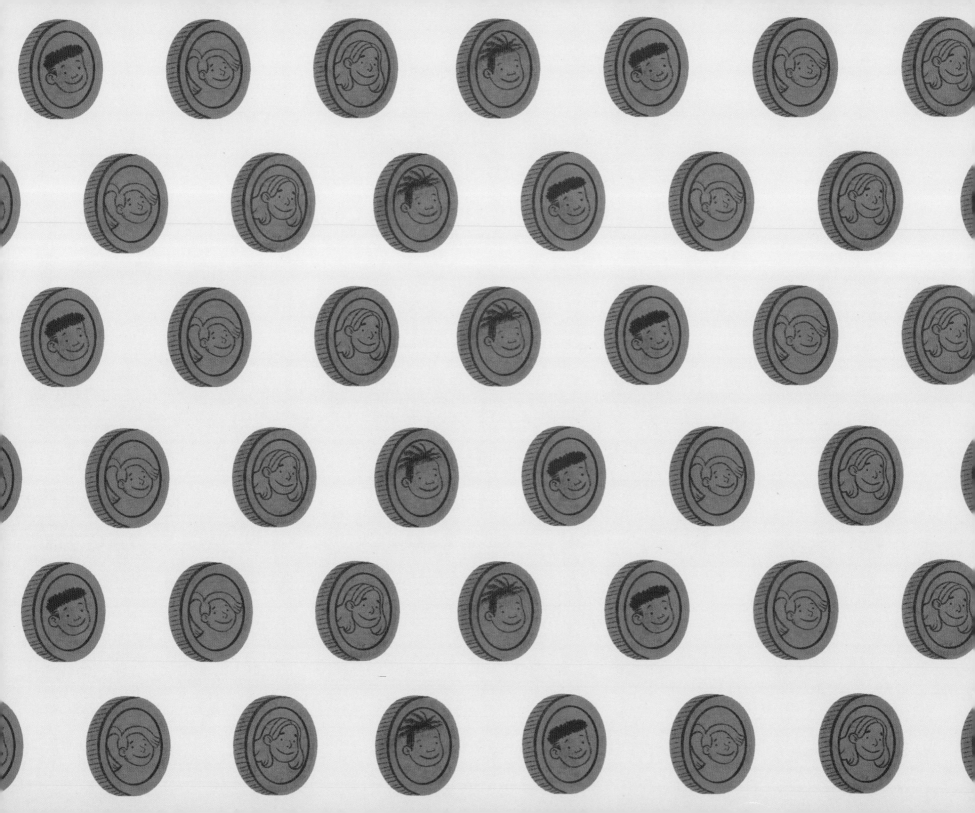